LEICESTERSHIRE

FOLK TALES FOR CHILDREN

LEICESTERSHIRE

FOLK TALES FOR CHILDREN

TOM PHILLIPS

First published 2018
Reprinted 2021

The History Press
The Mill, Brimscombe Port
Stroud, Gloucestershire, GL5 2QG
www.thehistorypress.co.uk

British Library Cataloguing in Publication Data.
A catalogue record for this book is available from the British Library.

ISBN 978 0 7509 8685 4

Typesetting and origination by The History Press
Printed and bound by TJ Books Limited, Padstow, Cornwall

Contents

About the Illustrators

Jenna Catton

Finding an illustrator seemed like it would be a big task. I had an idea in my head of what I wanted, and I wanted all my illustrations to be amazing. I am good enough at drawing myself but needed someone with great talent. However, I didn't find just one extremely talented illustrator, I found three! The first being Jenna.

Jenna is a storyteller as well as an illustrator. She comes from the West Midlands and has a style that I love. I found her through my storytelling friends and we hit it off straight away. She has worked really hard on producing the stunning artwork for the front cover, which is amazing.

Not only has she been doing the artwork, but she has been giving me pointers and suggestions whilst writing the stories. With the wonderful Internet making sharing my stories so easy, she has given me help and advice which I have valued greatly, as she is a wonderful storyteller herself.

You can find more of her work by searching for Jenna Catton Illustrations online.

Fern Brimley

I had told my mum that I was looking for illustrators for my new book. She mentioned it to a friend whose daughter was at university and friends with a girl who was a great artist and wanted to become an illustrator (did you get that?). Anyway, through one thing and another

I found myself with a name and a number and gave her a ring, not knowing anything more about her than this.

Well, Fern was very excited about having the chance to provide some illustrations for my book. I received some of her artwork over email and knew straight away that her art style was going to be perfect for a lot of my stories. Fern latched onto the darker, sadder stories and began working on those. The pictures she produced were beautiful and haunting. I couldn't be more pleased with them.

Fern is hoping this will be a step in the right direction towards achieving her dream of being an illustrator. I really hope she does, she is incredible.

Claire Alexandra

It's funny how you can know someone for ten years and still never really know them. It's also funny how what you need can be sitting under your nose all along, but you are too blind to smell it.

I went to university to study to be a teacher with Claire. We were never close friends but stayed in touch on the Internet all these years. I found myself struggling to get another illustrator. Jenna was working hard on the cover art, Fern was flat out with the inside illustrations for half the stories and her university work, but who was going to do the other pictures? I needed a bit of light to go with Fern's wonderful dark, and then I saw it.

On social media one day, I saw some brilliantly bright and light pictures painted by Claire. In a flash, I got in touch and asked her if she would like to do some art for my book. She told me she had put the paintbrushes down after university and had only just picked them back up. After reassuring her that I loved her work and I definitely wanted her to do some artwork, she sprang to it! Within days she had done several illustrations, pushing herself and producing some truly wonderful pictures.

I am truly very lucky to have such talented illustrators working for me. Please keep a look out for their work in future, you never know, this could be the start of big things for them. I honestly hope it is, they are awesome.

Are you Sitting Comfortably?

Hello and thank you. If you are reading this, then you are a very wise and clever person. You know how exciting and important local folk tales are, well done. You are probably wondering who I am, though. Well, my name is on the front cover, Tom Phillips, but I go by many names: Mr Phillips (when I was a teacher), Daddy (by my children), but the one most people may know me by is Tom the Tale Teller.

I have always had a love of stories and can remember my daddy reading me Brer Rabbit stories when I was a child. These folk tales had been passed down from the slaves of the Deep

South of America and were always about a quick-thinking rabbit outsmarting Brer Fox and Brer Bear. As I grew up, I found I loved hearing stories of places. I couldn't get enough of the stories from my village, Gilmorton, in the sleepy south of Leicestershire (you will find these stories later on in this book).

When I finally grew up (well, my body did, I still think of myself as a big kid at heart) I became a primary school teacher. I found myself telling all manner of stories to my classes, which they loved. I soon realised I had a gift for telling stories without books or scripts, just me, a story and an audience. I began telling stories all over the country to audiences young and old. I finally left teaching to become a storyteller. I travelled around, doing what I loved, all the time taking every opportunity to listen to other storytellers, to learn how they did it, to learn the stories they shared so I could bring that all together to make my own style.

Whilst doing all of this, I was writing. I was writing short stories for younger children that I hope I can get published one day. I also began writing my first big story, my novel. It was an idea I had had for many, many years and I finally started to put it down on paper. Thankfully, a bit of luck struck. I found myself being asked to write this book! I was over the moon!

As I said, I love local stories, and this gave me an excuse to find lots more of them. I have worked hard over the last few months to find stories from all over Leicestershire, some that have been written down before in other books for grown-ups, and some that have never been written down. I have played with them in my head, told some of them to audiences and finally wrote them down. I then read them over, changed bits, added bits, sometimes started again until, well, here we are, I finished them!

I really hope you enjoy them. I will have to warn you, though, Leicestershire seems to have a large number of rather spooky stories.

Some of these stories may be a bit scary, but remember this: scary stories are told to us so we learn how to control our fears. A story is just a story. Being scared by a story is a good thing as we know it is not real and we learn that being scared is OK.

These stories have been written to be enjoyable whether they are read aloud to you or you read them in your head. Some are short, some a bit longer and one chapter is full of short little nuggets of stories, more curiosities and interesting things than full stories. Read them, read them again, look at the pictures, live the stories and then head out into the wonderful landscape of Leicestershire with its rolling hills, rocky outcrops, babbling streams and sleepy villages, and find more stories.

1

King Leir

There once was a mighty king who ruled these lands long ago. His name was King Leir and he built his castle, from which he ruled, on the banks of the River Soar. He was the son of the great King Bladud and wanted, more than anything in this world, to father a son and heir to his throne.

King Leir was blessed with three children, only they were all girls. Three daughters, all three beautiful, all three smart. But this was not enough to stop the king from feeling disappointed. He did still love his daughters. More than anything, he loved his daughters.

The eldest was Goneril. She was headstrong, determined, and succeeded in all she did. She was as good with a bow as she was with the steps of the finest dances.

His second daughter was named Regan. Quick of temper and eager to please, she tried her hardest at all times, always trying to best her big sister in all they did.

The youngest was named Cordelia. She was a gentle girl, soft of voice and touch. She cared not for the bickering and competitions between her older sisters, but more for reading her books and walking along the riverside, listening to the birds and watching Mother Nature go about her business.

King Leir knew his time was running short. His girls were now all of an age to get married, and he was now an old man. His wife had died some years earlier and his thoughts had now turned to who he would give his kingdom to. Which of his three daughters would take his throne when he passed?

King Leir called the girls into his chambers. Goneril strode in first, elegant and refined. She was promptly pushed out of the way with a shoulder from her sister, Regan, who ducked under her elder sibling and was now in front. Last in the room was Cordelia, freshly picked herbs in her hand, having come from the kitchens where she had been cooking. The sweet, fragrant smell of rosemary and thyme filled the air and the king's nose and he smiled, his eyes closing for a brief second. He remembered his wife. She loved to cook. Her hands would always smell of fresh herbs and her hair of the finest of foods.

When the girls had lined up in front of their father, he looked them in the eyes and told them that, 'I am not getting any younger and soon I shall be gone.'

This caused all three girls to falter, none more so than Cordelia, who shed a tear down her delicate rosy cheek at the thought of losing her father.

The king continued. 'When this day comes, one of you will have to take my place and rule these fair lands. This will not be an easy choice, as I love each of you dearly and believe each of you would be a fine ruler of this land, so I must think carefully.'

The king stopped for a second. He gazed into each of his daughters' eyes, his heart filled with the love only a father could feel for these beautiful girls, and then asked, 'But first, tell me this: how much do you love me? You first, my dearest Goneril.'

Goneril stepped forward and fell at her father's right-hand side. 'I love you to the moon and back, Father, to the moon and back!' and with that she gazed up at him, fluttered her eyelids and gave a soft smile.

'And you Regan?' asked the king, raising his gaze towards the middle of his three daughters.

Always wanting to go one better than her sister, Regan flung herself to the floor on her father's left-hand side, clasped his hand tight and said, 'I love you to the sun and back, Father, to the sun and back (which is further than the moon … I think).'

Smiling down at both his eldest daughters the king's heart nearly burst out of his chest. Surely he could not take any more of this, he thought. But, nevertheless, he asked his youngest, the sweet Cordelia, 'And finally, my sweet, how much do you love me?'

Cordelia looked at the herbs in her hand, then up at her father, and thought hard. After a moment or two she spoke, 'I love you like fresh meat loves salt,' she said, smiling softly.

The king was confused. This was not what he was expecting. He saw this as a joke, no, an insult! He flew into a fit of rage. 'Guards!' he cried. 'Take her from my sight, she is banished from this land! She is no longer my daughter and therefore shall receive nothing from me and will never, EVER sit on this throne! How dare you insult me!' The king's face was redder than a tomato.

Swiftly, the guards did as they were ordered. Cordelia was dragged from the castle, thrown onto a cart and taken to the south coast, where she was hurled on board a merchant ship bound for France. She had been banished, cast out, forgotten by her whole family.

With the help of his loving and doting older daughters, the king calmed down. They poured gentle, soft words into his ears to cool his temper and sweeten him up. When his rage had dampened the king decreed that half his lands were to be given to his remaining two daughters now and, upon their marriage and his death, the remaining land was to be shared between them to rule separately as they saw fit.

But what of Cordelia? She had been left to wander in a foreign land. She was still dressed in the fine princess dress she had been wearing that fateful day. Realising she was a target for ruffians and thieves, she set to work. Sitting by a river she began gathering rushes. She wove these into a cloak and hood which she wore over her finery. Cordelia wove until her fingers bled and the disguise was finished. Gazing upon her reflection in the river, she thought that even her own father would not have been able to recognise her.

Cordelia wandered many miles, until she found a fine palace where there lived a prince. Desperate for food, she took herself to the kitchen door and begged the cook for work in return for scraps. The cook looked at this bedraggled sight, a scruffy girl wearing clothes made of rushes, and told her she could scrub pans and clean the kitchen for food and somewhere warm to sleep – but she must not leave the kitchen as the prince should not have to look upon such a sight as her.

'Come on then,' ordered the cook, 'you've got a job, now get to work Cap O'rushes, or whatever your name is.'

This name stuck, and Cordelia was now known as Cap O'rushes. She spent her days cleaning and her nights curled up asleep by the fire in the soot and cinders. It was a simple life, but she did not complain.

'Cap O'rushes, 'ave you 'eard?' squealed the chambermaid one day in utter excitement. 'The prince is holding a ball in three days' time so as he may find him a wife! I can't wait to see all those beautiful dresses.' She looked longingly into the middle distance, daydreaming of what she would see.

Come the night of the ball, the cook and the chambermaid finished their jobs and left to go and see the splendour of those at the ball. Cap O'rushes said she was not interested by those richer than her and chose to have an early night. However, when all had left the kitchen, she slipped off her tattered cloak and cap to reveal the wondrous dress she had been wearing when she had been banished from her homeland. A quick brush down and comb of the hair and she was ready.

Into the ballroom swept a vision of beauty, with the most dazzling red ringlets framing a soft, delicate face. The prince's eyes caught sight of her within an instant, and his heart began to pound so hard it felt as though it would burst out of his chest if he did not grab the girl and dance with her right now. And that is what he did.

The two danced until the room became empty and the music stopped, their eyes never once leaving each other's gaze, their lips never

once uttering a word. But then, the girl turned
and fled, out of the door and into the night.
'Wait! Come back!' cried the prince, but it was
no good.

Next morning, Cap O'rushes was yawning
an awful lot for someone who had supposedly

had an early night, not that the chambermaid noticed. She was too busy talking on and on about the ball, the dresses and the beautiful girl the prince danced with all night. 'And, rumour is, he is holding another ball next week in the hope the girl will be there, so as he may dance with her again,' finished the maid.

Cap O'rushes said nothing, but went about her jobs with a soft smile on her face and the rushes hiding her true self.

A week later, once more a ball and once more the girl with the red hair. Once more the prince danced with her until the people went home and the music stopped, and once more he forgot to ask her name until she had disappeared into the night.

And so it was that a third ball was held and everything happened as before. The girl, the dancing, the music stopping but, this time, the prince asked her what her name was so as he could find her again. 'I cannot tell you that my prince,' replied Cordelia, fearing the prince did not truly love her.

'But why?' pleaded the prince.

'For I fear this is just a fairy tale and no more. How do I know that I mean as much to you as you say?' challenged Cordelia.

The prince pulled out a ring and pressed it into her hand. 'I will look for you and when I find you, show me this ring to prove you are my true love.'

After that day, the prince searched the kingdom but with no luck. He could not find his true love anywhere. He became ill and took to his bed, suffering from a broken heart. When news of this reached the kitchen and Cap O'rushes, she knew his love for her was real and she smiled to herself.

Upstairs had requested a broth for the poorly prince, and Cap O'rushes insisted she made it for him. After much arguing, the cook agreed. Into the broth, Cap O'rushes slipped the ring. The cook presented the broth to the prince and, as he finished it, he spied the ring. He looked at the cook, a plump, older lady and asked, 'Who made this?'

'Well, I did, of course,' replied the cook, not wanting the prince to know she had let the cleaner do it.

'Tell me the truth,' the prince snapped, knowing this could not be the same girl he danced with and gave this very ring to. 'It was not you who made this, was it?'

'No, your highness,' answered the cook, 'it was the cleaner, Cap O'rushes, but I didn't think you …'

'Send her to me, now!' demanded the prince.

In a trice, she was there, in front of the prince. Cap O'rushes shed her rushes like a butterfly emerging from a cocoon and the prince finally saw her. The two sat and talked for hours and with each passing hour the prince gathered more strength. He learnt the girl's true name, where she came from and how she found herself so far from home. Over time they became married and life was good for Cordelia.

But what of her father, King Leir? He had found himself in rather a bad way. Goneril and Regan had married wealthy gentleman, who had both grown tired of waiting for their father-in-law to die and hand over the lands to them. So, they had mounted an attack on the king's palace on the River Soar and driven him out, claiming the lands for themselves. The king, feeling betrayed by the two daughters he thought loved him the most, now had no choice but to flee over the water to France.

The handsome prince Cordelia had married was now the king, and she sat beside him as queen. She had grown so much that, when Leir came to their palace asking for help, he did not recognise his own daughter.

He was invited to dine with them that evening, but Cordelia asked her old friend, the cook, to not put salt on any of the meat before or after cooking. The food was presented and what a fine banquet it was! The finest of foods, and the best cuts of meat. Leir's mouth watered. He sank his teeth into the finest cut of beef on the table but, well, it did not taste right. He sampled some of the lamb and the pork, but they seemed strangely bland too. It was then he realised they had not been seasoned, they needed … SALT!

Leir broke down in tears. He realised, only now, what his precious young daughter had meant all those years ago. 'How could I have been so foolish?' he sobbed into his hands.

He felt a hand rest gently on his shoulder and a soft, delicate voice say, 'It's alright Father, I forgive you, for I will always love you as fresh meat loves salt.'

Leir spun his head around. How could he not have realised this was his sweetest Cordelia! The two grabbed hold of each other and hugged as tight as bears, neither ever wanting to let go again.

With this reunion, and the hearts healed, the King of France, King Leir's new son-in-law, pledged his armies to his wife's father. They set sail the very next day, over the Channel, to Cordelia's homeland. There, with the might of the French army at his back, King Leir reclaimed his throne and his rightful position as King of England.

From the castle in which he ruled the land, there grew a great city, draped along the banks of the River Soar. This city was forever named after its founder and king, and was known as Leir's city. Over time, it changed to the form we now know as Leicester. But, even today, with the wonderful variety of restaurants and places to eat, from English to Indian, Turkish to Chinese, they all share one important cooking practice in common. They all know how much meat loves salt, and so season the meat to perfection.

2

Bel the Giant

Many years ago, in the time before Christians brought the word of their God to the shores of England, the people believed in many gods. They believed in the gods of the earth, the water, the sky. They believed in the gods of the plants, the forests and the seasons. For each, a different god, and they would pray to them and show them respect in the hope that these gods would be kind to them.

There were two very important gods that the people prayed to more than any other. These were the god of summer and the goddess of winter. They would pray to Bel for a good summer, warm and wet, to make the crops grow tall and the fruit nice and tasty. As for winter, they would pray to Danu for her to make the winter gentle and kind, with no big storms or heavy snow as this would make surviving harder. For each of these gods, the people would throw a party at the start of their season. They would light a fire, two large haystacks, and, if it was summertime, they would drive their animals in-between them and into the fields. If it was winter, they would drive them back through them, back into the people's houses where they would spend the winter, nice and warm and dry. For both of these celebrations the people ate lots of food and made offerings to the gods. The summertime celebration was known as Beltane, in honour of the summer god, Bel. We still celebrate it today but call it May Day. The winter celebration they called Samhain (said like this: SAH-win), which we now call harvest or Halloween.

These two gods were linked. Danu was a beautiful woman, who many believed was the first god there ever was. She was in love with Bel. Bel was a giant of a man, standing taller than any house the people of the land could build. Bel would appear at the beginning of summer from the frozen north, a young man in appearance. He travelled to where he would meet his love, Danu, every year on the same day. This place was the centre of what is now Leicester, not far from the clock tower. When the two met, they spent their time together enjoying the summer sun and each other's company. However, as the summer faded and autumn began to take hold, Bel would age. As trees drooped and dropped their leaves, ready to sleep through the winter, so too did Bel. With the first frosts of winter, he said his tearful goodbyes to his one true love, Danu, and travelled, slowly, north, now an old man. Once there, he would curl up in a long-forgotten cave and sleep, like a bear. Danu became sad. She had lost her love for another winter and, with her sadness, her heart became as cold as the north wind that now brought the snow and her skin would turn as blue as she felt. With her sadness, the winter took hold.

Up in the north, a strange thing would happen. Deep inside that forgotten cave, the sleeping giant, Bel, would shrink. He changed, much like a caterpillar changes into a butterfly. Bel became a small baby, sleeping soundly, growing with each passing winter's day. By the time spring had sprung, and the first daffodils had opened their heads and bowed to the sun, Bel was now a teenager. He would wake from his sleep and set off on the long journey south to see his love. By the time he arrived in Leicester, he was a fully grown giant of a man. Bel and Danu were happy once more. Danu lost her blue skin, and so the cycle of the year went on. Life, for now, was good for these gods.

Time had passed, like a wheel turning, the years had spun around many times and now a new religion had come to our shores. The Romans had found Britain. With them they brought many things: toilets, roads, medicine, education and policing. One of these things was a new god, *the* God. They believed Him to be the one and only god. The people of this land listened to what the Romans had to say and started to question if their gods were real. They started to challenge their gods to prove to them they were real gods. And so it was that this happened to Bel.

It was the start of summer and Bel was striding towards Leicester, a huge grin on his face, for he was going to meet Danu, his one true love! His strides were long, so long that he could step over many fields at once. When Bel was about 3 miles away from the centre of Leicester and his love, he was stopped by a group of men. They had to crane their necks to look up at him and shout very loudly for their voices to reach the giant's ears. Bel stopped, smiled at the little men and bent down to hear them.

'Good day, fine little sirs,' boomed Bel, his voice bouncing off the rolling hills round about, 'what a mighty fine day it is. How can I help you?' His face beamed like the sun, his cheeks rosy, his eyes sparkling.

The men jostled and shoved each other until one stepped forward (with a little helpful nudge). 'Oh great and powerful Bel, we have heard from the people that came on the ships to this land from far away that we are wrong, that there is only one God and that you and your kind are not really gods.' The man shouted this as loud as he could but he found it hard to control the nervous tremble in his voice.

'HA HA HA!' Bel's laughter shook the ground and moved the clouds. 'Do they now!' he said, once he had stopped his laughing.

'Yes, they do,' replied the man, 'and we are not sure if we believe them. Can you prove you really are a god?'

Bel's smile began to fall. Wrinkles the size of valleys appeared on his forehead. 'If I was not a real god, would I have me a beast as beautiful and mighty as this?' Bel responded. Placing two fingers as thick as branches in his mouth, he whistled. The sound pierced the air, and off in the east the men saw a huge brown horse, a sorrel mare, galloping over field and hill. The mighty creature came to a halt next to Bel, flicking its head down and shaking its mane.

'Well?' questioned Bel, his face now beaming with delight.

The men looked on in awe and wonder but then began to try and shake it off. 'That is impressive,' bellowed the man, 'but that proves nothing, only that you have a horse. I have a horse, albeit not that big.' He turned to his friends, who all laughed. 'To prove you are a god,' continued the man, 'we want to see you leap to the centre of Leicester in just three bounds.'

'Can I ride my horse?' asked Bel.

'If you must,' replied the man.

Three miles, three leaps. This was a big task, even for a god with a mystical giant beast, but Bel accepted the challenge.

Bel looked all around and found a nearby hillside, just perfect for him to use as a mounting post. Standing one foot on this rocky outcrop, he swung the other leg over the animal and mounted the sorrel horse. The men were impressed.

Bel whispered words into the horse's ears, words of encouragement and instruction. Bel then dug his heels sharply into the mare's hind-quarters. The horse rose up on her back legs and leapt forward. She soared through the air with her giant rider on her back. They landed, with one leap, nearly a mile and a half from where they left.

'Come on girl,' whispered Bel, 'you can do it! I believe in you!'

The men struggled to catch up but, when they did, they saw something amazing. Once more the sorrel mare flew into the air and leapt, but not as far this time. The first jump had taken too much from her. This time the effort was so great that, when the horse landed, her muscles burst from the force, her lungs burst from breathing so deeply and her heart burst from trying to pump the blood around her body so fast. They were now just 1 mile away from the centre of Leicester, from where Bel's true love, Danu, sat waiting, but the poor beast had given everything she could and all inside her had burst.

The men caught up with the horse and its rider just in time to see the horse rise up one more time. Bel was telling the courageous animal she did not need to do it, but the horse did not listen. Bel hung on tightly as the horse managed one final leap. The horse, once more, with all inside her burst, failed to jump the distance needed. She fell to the floor, throwing her rider as she did so, and died.

Bel was flung through the air and, when he landed, he struck his head upon a rock. The impact killed the mighty giant, instantly. As the life faded from his body, the light faded from his face. When the men caught up with Bel they looked upon him and cried. All light had gone from his face. The happiness this giant had was now lost from this world forever. With sorrow, the men realised what they had done. It did not matter whether or not Bel was a true god, what had mattered was the light his joy of living brought to the world. This giant only had a short time each year to live as a full-grown man and he made the most of it, bringing laughter and light to the world, and now these men had snuffed out that light forever.

They felt guilty over what they had done and decided to do the right thing. They took up their tools and began to dig. They dug a grave, big enough for Bel, and rolled him into it. There he lies still.

In honour of this wonderful giant of a man, the men decided to rename the places they had been. Where Bel mounted his sorrel mare became known as 'Mount Sorrel'. Where the duo had landed after their first leap was called 'One Leap' (Wanlip). The place where all inside the horse burst was renamed 'Burst all' (Birstall), and finally, the resting place of this great man 'Bel's Grave' (Belgrave).

These names were never forgotten, and it is up to you now to never forget the story behind them. So, next time you are around the north-west of Leicestershire, keep an eye out for those names, for the rocky hill at Mount Sorrel, and remember the great god Bel.

But what of the seasons, you may ask? Well, they rolled on, that great wheel still spinning as it always has, as it always will do. And what about Danu, sat there waiting for her true love? Well, these are questions you may find answers to in another story.

3

The Griffin of Griffydam

Many tales are told throughout the land of how strange place names came about. Here, in Leicestershire, is no exception, as you have just seen. Some of the stories explain unusual names but some, like the small hamlet of Griffydam, in north west Leicestershire, require the use of your imagination.

Back in the times when Charnwood was still a wood, with trees stretching as far as the eye could see and only the occasional peaks poking out of the sea of green, there were many small hamlets. These sprang up in clearings and, usually, near a water source, whether it be a spring or stream. Griffydam was no different, only, back then, it was known by a different name, one long forgotten nowadays.

This land was looked over by the monastery that perched like an eagle on top of the highest peak, Breedon Hill. Breedon Priory was the centre of all life for those living within walking distance. This is where they would go and pray every Sunday. No matter how long the walk, the people would make it to a service every week, without fail. The monks that lived there were kindly and wise, and so it was to them that the people of a nearby hamlet turned when trouble came knocking at their door.

A young boy had been sent to the well just outside of the village, to collect some water for his family. As he rounded the trees on the path, there in front of him he saw the stone structure that the village had built, some years ago, to pool the fresh spring water, making it easy to fill the buckets. On a normal day, the young boy would have to plunge the buckets into the pool of water, fill them up and carry them up the path to home. On a normal day, this would be his first chore of the day. On a normal day, there wouldn't be a hulking beast sat on the well!

The boy froze. His heart stopped. His jaw dropped. There in front of him, lying draped over the well, damming the water, was a terrifying beast. His eyes darted over the creature as he tried to hold his breath. It was like some great and powerful being had merged two of the most vicious animals together to create something that would haunt anybody's dreams. The creature's body was as large as the carts the villagers used to carry wool or bricks, which they made in the village, to and from the market in the local town. It was covered in the finest fur, a rich golden orange, like the wheat in the fields in summer. It had four legs, each as thick as a small tree, the back two with paws at the end, the front with talons like those of a bird. Out of these paws and talons sprang claws the size of daggers. The boy's gaze wandered from the muscled body to the head. The fur stopped, and the feathers began. Silky brown and white they were, capping the head of an eagle, a large smoky orange beak, pointy and powerful, erupting from it. The creature's eyes were tight shut, his head curled around and resting partly under two humongous wings that sprouted out of its back.

Seeing the creature was asleep, the boy began to tiptoe slowly backwards until he rounded the trees. He spun on his heels and ran, leaving the buckets were he dropped them. Breathless, he flew into the village, shouting about what he had seen. The villagers gathered around and all began frowning and chuntering to each other, not believing the boy but, after some persuading, they agreed to follow him back to the well.

There was no denying it now, the beast was there, plain to see to all the villagers, and they all felt the same heart-stopping fear the boy had that first time of seeing it. They all fled quickly back to the village. A meeting was called in the meeting house and they discussed what was to be done. The beast must be moved or they would run out of water. The nearest water source was many miles away. Something had to be done!

The first idea was for the villagers to try and drive this beast away. They armed themselves with axes, daggers, pitchforks and whatever they could find. They were a peaceful village, living in peaceful times, and so had no need for weapons. The bravest of the men walked down the path to the well. They rounded the corner and saw the creature. Brandishing their makeshift weapons, they approached. The creature heard them coming and opened its yellow eyes. The men jumped backwards. A few were brave enough to prod at the beast but these attacks were of no use. The creature batted them away like a cat playing with a ball of string, breaking the weapons and sending the men flying through the air. They gathered themselves together and all beat a hasty retreat. They realised this creature was more than they could deal with.

Next day was Sunday, a day of worship. The villagers made their way to the priory, and after prayers had been said, they spoke to the eldest and wisest of the monks about their problem.

'You have a griffin,' came the answer in a voice like sandpaper from the wise old monk. 'This is a rare and wonderful creature, part eagle, part lion. They are usually docile and calm unless attacked.'

'We know, we found that out the hard way,' came a chorus of voices in response.

'They are also fearfully protective of what they think is theirs, in this case, your well,' explained the monk.

'So what do we do about it then?' asked the now desperate villagers.

'There is nothing much you can do,' replied the monk to a very disappointed-looking crowd, 'other than wait and pray it leaves soon.'

And so it was, the villagers left with their hearts heavy and their hopes dashed. Life was going to get harder from hereon in.

After a week, as luck would have it, a knight came riding through the village. His armour was polished until it reflected even the faintest of light. He had been riding for many hours and needed a drink. He had heard this village had a spring and the water from it was the finest in the land. The villagers refused him water as they were running low and explained their problem. The knight mounted his steed, turned down the road and set off towards the well. 'I will slay this beast!' he announced loudly.

A buzz ran through the village. As the people heard the news they flocked out of their houses and followed the knight, like

sheep, down the road. The knight on his horse, and the villagers on foot, rounded the trees and saw the griffin, sleeping once more. Leaping from his steed, the knight drew his sword and was about to charge at the creature when the villagers held him back. 'Wait,' they said, 'we've tried that. He is too strong, even for a noble knight like you.'

For a minute the knight stood and rethought his strategy. He walked to his horse, then took in hand his longbow and a single arrow before turning towards the griffin. He walked around the creature so that he was face to face with it, some distance away, so as to not get caught by its impressive beak. The knight began to shout. 'Hey, you foul beast, will thee not wake and fight me!'

The griffin opened his eyes, took one look at the knight, and turned his head. One shiny man was not worth the effort, it thought.

'I was talking to you, do not be so rude. I am a knight of the realm!' continued the knight.

Once more the griffin opened its eyes and, this time, raised its head to assess this threat. The griffin may have been a beast, but it could understand every word the knight was saying. It was just about to put its head down and close its eyes once more when the knight shouted, 'So, you are a cowardly beasty then!' laughing as he did so.

The griffin's gaze fixed now on the knight; he was angered. He opened his beak and shouted in reply, 'Me not a beasty, me a misunderstood birdy!' and followed this with an ear-splitting shriek.

With his beak now fully open, the knight knocked the arrow, drew it to his chin, took aim and loosed it. The arrow flew through the air and found its mark, right inside the griffin's mouth. The knight had rightly guessed that an arrow into its side would do no good, those wings gave too much protection. It was like the griffin had its own suit of armour. The knight had found a soft spot, the fleshy back of its mouth. It worked. In an instant the griffin's head dropped and he was dead.

That night, much celebrating was had and much water was drunk, now the griffin had been removed from the well. It was said that the griffin was hung above the door of the priory. If so, it is not there now, only a carving of one in the ruins.

And so it was, the village was forever known as the place the griffin dammed the well, or Griffydam for short.

4

Danu

We have all heard of child-eating witches. Hansel and Gretel run into one who lives in a gingerbread house, Baba Yaga lives in a hut on giant chicken legs that walks around the forests of Russia, but did you know there is one right here, in Leicestershire, living beneath your very noses? If you dare to find out more then read on, but beware: you might not sleep so soundly in your beds tonight.

Long ago, the great goddess, Danu, brought warmth and love to this world. She would spend her summers in the arms of her beloved, the great giant god Bel. She was happy. Her hair was golden like the corn in the field, her skin pale and soft. Summer was good for the great Danu. But then the time came, as it did every year, when Bel became tired and needed his sleep and so left her. He travelled north whilst Danu stayed in the rolling hills of Leicestershire. Her skin would turn blue, her hair as black as night and the icy cold of her heart would grip the lands all about and bring winter. This way she would stay until her true love returned to her in the spring, when she would once more be fair of hair and pale of skin and the warmth returned to her heart.

And so the cycle went on, and on, and on, until one year, when the men of the land tricked her beloved and he fell to his death. This enraged Danu! Her blood boiled and her skin turned red for a time. She spent many nights thinking how she could get her revenge for what the men of this land had done to her beautiful Bel. As she fixed on one goal, on one

single thought, revenge, her eyes began to move closer together until they met in the centre of her forehead and formed but one. This eye turned a dark blood red, reflecting the single thought she had set her mind to.

She was saddened greatly, too, by Bel's death, and that sadness showed on her skin as it started to fade, from the fiery red it had become, to a deep, cold, icy blue.

Finally, she had a plan. The men of this land had taken what she loved most in this world from her, so she would take what they loved most. Not their wives, but their children! Danu grew her nails until they were more like talons. She then melted down iron ore over a great fire and plunged her fingernails into this. As the liquid metal hardened, she was left with giant metal claws on the ends of her blue, bony fingers. She would spend hours grinding and sharpening these until they shone with even the faintest of light and could split a hair from your head in two.

Danu began stalking the lands around Leicester, taking children in the dead of night. If they were foolish enough to be out past dark, then Danu would have them for her own. She would take their skins to wear around her like a skirt and eat what was left. Rumour began to spread of this creature, blue of face, red of eye, ironclad claws and a hunger for children. Her name was not known by the men of the land so many names sprang up, all referring to her black cloak which she wrapped around herself to hide in the inky black of the shadows. Of all the names, Black Annis was the one that stuck in the minds of the families in the lands to the west of Leicester. By now, Danu had embraced her new name and had clawed herself a cave from the rocks in the Dane Hills, close to where Weston Park now lies. Above this cave, which the locals called Black Annis's Bower, stood an ancient oak tree. In this she would hide, watching and waiting for any child who

dared come too close, so she may drop on them like an eagle on its prey.

As time passed, her name became myth, folklore, a story parents told their children to make sure they would return home before dark, for fear of Black Annis finding them. Mothers telling their children as they huddled in bed, their blankets pulled tightly up to their chins. But, as with all stories, we never fully believe them without the proof to back them up. And so it was that the once mighty goddess turned vengeful witch drifted out of our reality … or did she?

5

Black Annis

It was 1941. The war had been raging for nearly three years with no end in sight. Britain stood alone against the might of the Nazis and their leader, Adolf Hitler. Towns and cities were being bombed, night after night after night. Houses, streets and factories were being flattened. Families spent most nights huddled in basements or in freezing cold Anderson shelters in their gardens. The unlucky ones slept under their kitchen tables in reinforced cages called Morrison shelters or in the fireplaces or under the stairs for safety.

The government had started evacuating the children of these town and cities out to the quieter countryside. Thousands of children were carried away from their parents on trains and buses to live with families they didn't know and who may not have even wanted them. These families had no choice, it was the law that they had to have these evacuees. It was total potluck as to whether you got a nice family or a not-so-nice one.

Betty, John and Trevor had been lucky. They had been evacuated to the outskirts of the rarely bombed Leicester. They had ended up with an elderly couple, Mr and Mrs Potts. The three children, siblings, never found out if the Potts ever had children, they never spoke of them if they did and they would have been grown up now anyway. This aside, they were kind people. As long as the children did their chores and helped out around the house, they would be fed well and treated kindly. One job the three children got to do together was to collect bundles of wood from the nearby woodland, to feed the fire in the evening to help keep the little thatched cottage warm at night. It sat on the edge of the Dane Hills and looked out across the rolling countryside of west Leicestershire.

One day, they had all been busy with housework and suddenly realised the time. It was late October and the nights were now drawing in fast. It was mid-afternoon, and the shadows were growing when they remembered they hadn't been to collect wood for the fire.

'Come on boys, put a coat on, we've got one more job to do,' ordered Betty. She was the eldest, the bossy one, the mother hen.

'But I'm tired!' moaned the youngest, Trevor.

'And I'm hungry,' stated John, but that was no surprise, he was always hungry.

Just then, Mr Potts walked in the room and saw them putting on their coats. 'Where do you think you're going?' he questioned.

'Out to get firewood, we ain't done that yet,' answered Betty.

'Not now ya ain't, it's getting too late! Black Annis'll be about!' he replied.

John creased in two. 'She ain't real! She's just a story! An' we all know stories ain't true, Mr Potts.'

Betty smirked whilst Trevor forced a smile. Betty didn't believe the stories, but Trevor was not too sure.

Mrs Potts walked into the room, laid a hand on the shoulder of Mr Potts and, with the other, pulled something from her pocket. 'They'll be fine dear. They're smart and quick enough and we ain't seen 'ide nor 'air of 'er for ages. I'll give 'em this anyway, just in case.' She turned to the children. Into Betty's hand she pressed a smooth grey stone. Betty looked at it as Mrs Potts pulled her hand away. 'Take this, me duck, it'll come in 'andy.'

Betty could see the stone had a hole in it, one that had been worn out naturally. 'What's this?' she questioned, with a slight quiver in her voice. The way the two grown-ups were talking had unnerved her. Something wasn't right, she could tell.

'It's a hag stone, love. If ya 'ear anything unusual, anything at all, 'old this up and look through the 'ole. It reveals anything that doesn't want to be seen, like 'er.'

'Her?' asked John, butting in.

'Black Annis,' replied Mrs Potts.

'Enough of this,' cried Mr Potts. 'If ya going then go, but be back sharpish before it gets dark and pray you don't have to use that thing.'

The three children walked briskly through the woodland, arms filling with bundles of wood. They had been careful at first, checking all around, worried by the words of Mr and Mrs Potts. Now, however, those words and the warning seemed a distant memory. They enjoyed being in the trees. It wasn't like the endless terraced houses on the street where they lived with their mum and dad. As they were laughing and giggling, the shadows grew long, too long. They had failed to notice the sun start to slip beneath the horizon. The colours all around had started to drain in the half-light of dusk. There was a snap of a twig. It cut through the air like a hot knife through butter and the playful sounds of the children were silenced. The three of them froze. Their eyes darted all around, their hearts beating so fast they felt like they were about to burst through their chests. But nothing. The children could see nothing out of the ordinary. Nothing … except …

'What's that?' exclaimed John, pointing to the base of a large tree, now cast in shadow by the setting sun.

Betty, with Trevor now clasped like a limpet to her leg, gazed quizzically to where John's finger led. He was right, something was there, something that didn't belong.

'Use the stone!' whispered John, for fear of being heard. Trevor tugged Betty's skirt, stared up to her face and frantically shook his head, for fear of her seeing what he feared the most.

'It's all right,' came Betty's voice, soft and soothing, just like their mother's, 'it's nothing and I'm going to prove it by looking through this silly stone.' Secretly, she didn't believe a word of what she had just said, but needed to be brave for her brothers.

Betty raised the stone, closed one eye and peered through the hole. It was hard to focus through such a small hole. She scanned all around, her hand trembling, her breathing fast and her heart beating faster. On the first scan around she failed to notice anything out of the ordinary, but, when she scanned back around, as her gaze whipped past that tree she froze. She had seen something. She didn't want to believe she had seen anything, but she had. To be sure, she had to look back, but every bit of her body was telling her not to. She could feel Trevor's hands gripping tight onto her leg and then felt John's hand slip into her free hand.

She did it. She looked back at the base of the tree through the stone and, as she feared, there she was. The true horror was revealed. She could see clearly now, the magic unveiled. There, at the base of the tree, stooped over, was the figure of a woman. She was cloaked in black but an eerie blue glow shone from beneath. Her hands glistened with the last few rays of the fading light and Betty could make out metal claws.

'RUN!!!' she screamed at the top of her lungs.

The three children turned tail and ran. They scrambled towards the edge of the wood, towards safety, towards the house they now called home. As they ran, Trevor's foot found a tree root and he tumbled to the floor. Betty skidded to a halt, turned and ran back to grab him. In doing so, she caught sight of the now fully visible figure. This was Black Annis, there was no mistaking. As she gave chase, her hood had dropped to reveal that crimson red eye, the lurid blue skin and her patchy, straggly hair.

Betty dropped her bundle of wood, hoisted her brother up to his feet and the two of them took flight once more. The children heard a clatter and a screech. They turned briefly to see Black Annis in a heap on the floor, having fallen over the discarded wood. They did not stay still for long, though, and soon began to run once more.

They cleared the edge of the wood, but with each agonising step the evil hag got closer and closer. She was almost on their coat-tails now, nearly within striking distance.

They screamed at the house as they got nearer, for someone to open the door. As they entered the garden, through the picket fence, the wooden door flung open. It was bright, warm and so inviting inside. John bundled his way in first, closely followed by Betty dragging Trevor by the scruff of his neck. As they did, Black Annis pounced.

Into the doorway, putting himself between the children and the hag, appeared Mr Potts.

Black Annis froze, her single red eye staring into his dark brown ones. The children watched as, with hate and rage, Mr Potts raised up the hatchet he used for chopping wood and cried, 'Not this time ya old hag! Not these children! I won't let ya have these. You've taken too much from me, ya ain't havin' these!'

And with that, he brought the hatchet down heavy into the eye of Black Annis. Her screams were enough to curdle the blood in your veins and were heard as far off as Nottinghamshire, Derbyshire and Birmingham, or so it was said. The scream reminded the children of the air-raid sirens from back home but, whilst they signalled bad times, this scream was a sign of a joyous thing, the end of Black Annis. She turned and fled, hatchet still embedded in her eye, and that was the last anyone saw of her.

Today the house is gone. So too are the woodlands. The war came to an end and Leicester crept over the countryside, with new housing estates springing up here, there and everywhere. The Dane Hills are now covered in houses, streets and shops. Black Annis's bower now lies empty, almost forgotten, except for the people in whose garden it lies. And what of Black Annis?

Well, the people of the Dane Hills and Leicester have not reported seeing her since that night, but that is not to say she is gone forever. Remember, she was a goddess, and they are very hard to kill. She could still be lurking nearby, watching, waiting for some poor child to venture out of their house after dark and, when they do, she will be there.

But remember still, these are stories, folk tales, told to children to scare them, to make them come home by dark. It's not real … or is it?

6

The Oak and the Ash

If you were to take a trip to the tiny little hamlet of Peckleton in the south-west of the county, park up in Manor Lane, strap on your walking boots and take a stroll along the public footpath towards Earl Shilton, you would eventually come across a very peculiar tree. There, in the middle of a field, near a stream, stood not one, but two trees, growing together as one. An oak tree, wrapped around an ash tree. Two trees, merged together. A very odd sight to behold, but how did this come to be? If trees grow that close together, usually the quicker growing and the strongest would take all the goodness from the soil and the other would die. So how have two very large, very healthy trees grown so close to each other?

If you were then to speak to the locals, to ask them of this tree, they would tell you this story, a story of love, a story of loss and a story of never forgetting.

Back in the late 1700s, the land in the triangle between the hamlets of Peckleton, Earl Shilton and Kirkby Mallory was a patchwork of small fields. These were owned by just three families and had been for many, many years. They did not speak to each other and very much kept themselves to themselves.

'I don't trust them Peckleton folk, me. Always leaning on their tools, too busy looking at what we is doing, not working much on their own work,' the workers from Earl Shilton would say.

'Shifty lot, them over there. Beware of them. They make out that they are working but their eyes are flicking up and down from their work, watching us. I don't trust them I don't!' went the chatter from the Peckleton farmers.

'If they spent more time working and less time spying on each other, they'd be done in half the time!' the Kirkby Mallory folk would say about their neighbours.

Come evening time, after many hours working the fields, the families would return to their hamlets, to their taverns to drink ale and gossip about their neighbours, very much like we do, even to this day.

This particular year had started well for all three hamlets. The weather had been fair with spring showers helping the freshly sown crops to sprout. But the new crops were not the only things that had begun to grow that fine spring, for young love was in the air.

Early in the season, a young man from the Earl Shilton side of the valley looked up from his work to spy on those workshy Peckleton lot. But, to his utter delight, his eyes fell upon a vision of wonder. A young lady. She was leaning on her seeding tool, delicately dabbing beads of sweat off of her forehead. Her long, jet-black curls fell upon her shoulders and the delicate skin on her cheeks was flushed and rosy.

The young man's heart nearly burst from his chest! He had heard of love at first sight but thought this to be a load of codswallop. 'How can you fall in love with someone you have never met?' he would ask of anyone who challenged him on this. But, against his own beliefs, there he was, head spinning, knees wobbling, drool dripping from his chin. There was no doubt about it, this boy was in love!

On the other side of the valley, as she was gently mopping the hard work from her brow, the young lady lifted her eyes up and caught sight of a young man. He was funny. His hair was wild, his shoulders wide and he stood, staring straight at her. She felt a flutter in the pit of her belly and a smile push up the corners of her mouth and make her glowing cheeks dimple with delight. She, too, was in love.

And so the seasons rolled on, but such was the distrust and rivalry between the hamlets that the two lovers could not speak, only gaze at each other from afar and dream of a life where they could be together, forever.

Then the day came. It was late summer and the harvest was being chopped and brought in. The sun was high in the sky and the workers were hot. Their mouths were as dry as the parched soil beneath their feet. 'Boy!' shouted one of the workers to the young lover. 'Boy, stop leaning on your scythe and daydreaming and make yourself useful. Go to the stream and bring back some water for us to drink and cool our heads.'

The young man snapped out of his daydream, one filled with visions of the young lady working just over the valley. He lay down his scythe, picked up a bucket, and trudged down the valley side towards the stream. As he neared the water's edge, he spied an all-too-familiar face on the far side. As luck would have it, the young lady of his dreams, the one he was utterly in love with, was also collecting water. She too had been daydreaming as had he.

Now was his chance. As the young man bent to scoop the water, he whispered, 'I love you with all my heart. If you feel the same, meet me here when night has fallen.' The words fell softly from his mouth, bounced playfully over the ripples of the stream and nestled into the young lady's ears. For fear of getting in trouble, she said not a word but looked up with her green eyes and smiled. Green eyes. He'd not noticed this from afar, but this detail made the young man fall even more in love with her. He hoped and prayed she would be there that night.

Nightfall came. The sun dropped from the sky, but light clung on until the moon had risen and the blackness of night had driven away the day. The stream bubbled and burbled as a lone nightingale sang in the tree. The young man sat and waited. Would she come? Did she love him too? Had she told anyone of this forbidden meeting?

A shadow began to approach from the far side of the stream. The young man strained his eyes to see. Who was it? Was it her?

The shadow drew nearer, until he noticed it was the figure of a woman in a long dress. As she stepped out of the treeline and into the moonlight the young man's heart did a somersault. It was her! The young lady he had fallen for. He bounded over the stream and there they sat, and there they talked, and there they stayed until the sky turned bluey-grey and the sun began to wake.

Night after night the two of them met, there, in that field by the stream. Every night they met, and they became more and more in love. Summer turned to autumn, autumn to winter and still they would meet in that field. Shorter days meant longer nights for them to be together. They had made plans to run away together, maybe to London, to start a new life, together, forever.

On the first night of spring the two met as usual, but something was not right. The young lady looked worried. Her father had told her she was to marry a young man from Kirkby Mallory, so they would be able to merge the lands. Needless to say, the two were devastated. They sat and talked of what they would do. Could they run away? But, in the end, the young girl did not want to go against her father's wishes and, besides, they would always have this, their meetings together, although they would now have to stop.

The young man had an idea. He scooped up an acorn and told her to find a seed also. The young lady found a winged ash seed. They planted them carefully, next to each other, with as much love and care as they shared with each

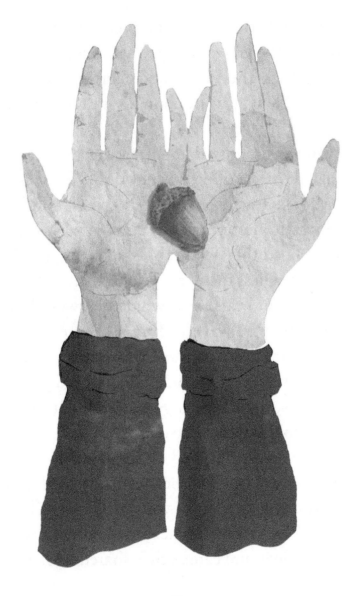

other. They promised to come back to this spot, but never on the same night, to care for and nurture their seeds and, in doing so, although they could never be together in life, they could always be together in spirit.

As the trees grew, the oak wrapped itself around the ash, protecting and loving it as the young man loved the young lady. And this is how they stood, the two trees, for many, many years. They were to be forever together, the young lovers whose love could never be.

However, whilst writing this book, one of my talented illustrators, Jenna, took the walk I described. She parked at the church, strapped on her walking boots and walked south along the footpath. I was sitting at home, only for my phone to ping. It was a picture message from Jenna. She had found the trees but something terrible had happened to the ash. We don't know what it was, but the farmer had had to chop it down. He did leave the oak standing. So now the mighty oak stands alone in their field,

his true love's branches no longer intertwined. But don't be saddened. Any tree you see is as big above the ground as it is below it. The ash tree's roots still run deep in and around the oak's, and will do so forevermore.

7

The Hermit of Holywell

There are many stories told about wells and springs with magical powers. Water that springs from the earth is a strange and wondrous sight and these places have been made into drinking wells, as with the well at Griffydam. This story is one of a well, not far from Griffydam, in the mystical area of Charnwood.

The night was dark and stormy. Clouds raced like giant ships across the sky. Flashes of lightning threw long, scary shadows across the ground. Agnes ran. She clambered over the razor-like rocks above Woodhouse Eaves and stumbled on towards the outwoods. Her pursuers were close behind and getting closer. It is hard to get away from someone when they are over twice your size. You see, the people chasing her were not ordinary people. They were the Comyns of Whitwick Castle.

The Comyns had lived in Whitwick Castle for many generations. They all stood well over twice the height of normal men. Some believed they were descendants of the mighty giant god Bel, but this was just rumour and hearsay, nothing but a folk tale. But we all now know, folk tales have some grain of truth resting inside them. Because of their height they were called giants and had seen fit to take whatever they fancied over the years. This particular year, Lord Comyn had taken a fancy to Agnes, a pretty young lady of Groby Castle. He had stridden over there and tried to seize her through one of the upstairs windows. Poor Agnes was terrified and took flight, running as fast as she could out of the back of the castle. However, it was some time before Lord Comyn realised his prize had slipped from his fingertips and out the back door, so the fair maiden had a good head start (which she needed). Lord Comyn and his men gave chase, each of their strides covering three of Agnes's.

Agnes knew she would be safe at the holy site of Grace Dieu Priory, for the monks would give her shelter and Lord Comyn was a God-fearing man, so he would not dare to try and take her from there. To get there, however, would mean going straight past Whitwick Castle, which was the last thing she wanted to do. Agnes headed north, through what is now Bradgate Park and on towards Woodhouse Eaves. There she started to travel north-west, through the outwoods. The night drew in, the darkness wrapped around her like a blanket and the heavy rain began to sting her eyes. She stopped. That was when she realised she was lost. She no longer knew north from south, east from west, even up from down! The one thing she did know was that Lord Comyn and his men were coming. She could hear the thudding of their boots on the ground in between the rumbles of thunder.

Not knowing what to do, tired, wet, hungry and thirsty, Agnes hid behind a mighty oak. She nestled between its ancient, gnarled roots and covered herself with fallen leaves. And there she lay, still, unmoving. She strained her ears to listen. She could hear the rain thundering on the leaves all around and the steady march of the pursuers' boots. As she lay with the spiders and worms, beetles and bugs, crawling into her clothes to share her warmth, Agnes began to say a prayer.

The boots came within touching distance of Agnes. She wanted to move, she wanted to jump up and rip the bugs from off her skin, but she stayed still. She held her breath as one of the giant men stood over her. Had he seen her? Then, he spun on his heels and his voice

boomed to the others, 'Nothing here lads, she's given us the slip. I'm soaked through and need some food, let's call it a night and go home.'

Agnes's heart fluttered with delight. She lay waiting until the giant men had gone. Then she tried to move. This was when the trouble started. She had been shivering from the cold but now she had stopped. Her body had gone numb. She found it almost impossible to move her arms and legs. With what little strength she had left, she hauled herself from out of her hiding place and dragged herself into the clearing nearby. There she stopped and flopped onto the ground.

The sun rose and chased the storm clouds away. First light of morning saw the emergence of the local hermit. This was a deeply religious man who had chosen to live on his own in the wilds, to spend his time praying, to be closer to God. In the mornings he would walk to the local priory of Grace Dieu to pray, before returning to his hovel for more prayer in the afternoon. This morning was no different. As he crossed the clearing he saw a young girl lying on the ground, wet as a drowned rat and as stiff as a statue. He rushed over and gently laid his hand on her forehead. She was stone cold. The life had long since left her body. It broke the hermit's heart to see such a tragic sight. Such a waste

of life and so young she was. He knelt beside
her and began to pray.

Then, as the morning sun peeked through the
branches and warmed his neck, the hermit had
an idea. 'Maybe, just maybe,' he thought. He
stood up, turned and ran to the nearby spring,
where the waters of the earth bubbled up out

of the ground. When he got there, he filled a jug as best he could and returned to the lifeless girl's body. Rolling her onto her back, he slowly poured the water between her lips and prayed once more.

The world seemed to hold its breath. Even the rustling trees fell silent for a brief moment. Then, coughing and spluttering, Agnes sat upright. She was alive! When she had come to her senses, she thanked the hermit for what he had done for her and explained all that had happened. The hermit took her to seek refuge at the priory where she was welcomed with open arms. After saying his morning prayers, the hermit returned to his home.

One year later, as the hermit was leaving for his morning walk to the priory, a young man and lady stopped on their horses. They dismounted and the young man began to shake the hermit's hand. 'Thank you, oh thank you, you marvellous man,' the young man exclaimed. 'If it wasn't for you, my wife would never have survived that dreadful night, would never have found me and we would never have been married.'

The hermit looked closer at the young lady and, sure enough, he recognised her to be that very same woman he had restored to life a year ago. His face beamed with a smile as she hugged him and whispered thank yous in his ear. The young man explained that he was Edward Grey (maybe a relation to Lady Jane Grey, we do not know) and that, as a thank you, they would gift the hermit three deer each year. Alongside this, the hermit was also granted the lands around the well, so he may look after it and live there in peace for the rest of his life.

8

The Nine O'Clock Horses

Switch out your light, come kiss me good-night, the nine o'clock horses are taking flight.

The city had started to grow. It swelled like the belly of a beast after a large feast. People were moving out of the countryside and into the city to find work in the factories. Gone were their nice country cottages. Gone were their gardens. Gone was the space and freedom, but they had

jobs, they had money, they had the nine o'clock horses.

In the late 1800s, Leicester was a dirty place. The drains could not cope with all the people flocking into the city. Animal and human waste was being dumped into the streets, flowing down the hills and into the River Soar. The streets were narrow and, even in the daytime, light was hard to find. When darkness crept across the land, the gas lamps were lit. Men dressed in black, with long wicks in hand, passing from lamp to lamp. The sickly yellow light, barely reaching the ground in which the street lamps stood. Murky mists filled the air, found the nooks and searched out the crannies, bringing a strange, unearthly feel to the city streets.

'If you're not in bed by nine o'clock, the horses will come and take you away, never to be seen again!'

the mothers would warn their children. You may think this a story, just an old yarn spun to make the children go to bed with no fuss or bother, but you'd be wrong. As the bells of the churches and the cathedral rang through the pea soup of the streets and alleyways, the muffled silence was cut through by the sound of metal on cobble. Horses' hooves sparked on the stones and their whinnying and neighing slipped through the gaps in the doors and windows and poured into the children's ears. There they lay, still, silent. Ragged covers clasped around their chins, praying this would not be the night the horses took them away.

Young Ethel lay like this. It was a particularly horrid night. All day it hadn't gotten much lighter than at dawn, thick heavy cloud and the smoke from the factories blocking the autumn sun from bringing light or warmth. Now, with the fall of night, no stars twinkled, no sign of the moon, just black skies and misty, acrid smog outside her window.

Ethel shared her parents' bed. She was the only child left at home, although she'd had a younger brother and older sister once. Her younger brother was lost to the family when he was a baby. He got sick and passed away, such was the case in those days. Her older sister had been sent away to work when she turned twelve. Now, there were just the three of them. They lived in a house with only two rooms, one bedroom upstairs and one living area downstairs in which they cooked, ate and lived.

That night the distinctive chime of the cathedral bells rang out, choked by the mists. Ethel counted the chimes. She counted nine. Her heart began to lurch. She could hear the blood pumping through her ears, thrum, thrum, thrum. It was only minutes but seemed like hours that she lay there, listening, straining to hear anything, anything out of the ordinary. Then it came. The metallic clank of horseshoe on stone. A steady clip-clopping of horses down her road. Occasionally they would stop, and the clip-clopping would be replaced by a scraping, and then the hooves began moving again, closer and closer. Would this be the night they came for Ethel? Had she shut her curtains tight enough? Will they see?

Ethel glanced towards the window and, in the darkness, she could see a sliver of gaslight prising its way through a crack in the curtain. Ethel's heart jumped into her mouth. This was the night! This was the night the nine o'clock horses noticed her and took her away!

Should she close the curtains? Or, should she stay where she was, pulling the covers over her head and hoping they would walk on by? Her mind spun.

She felt her legs swing out of bed and she dashed towards the curtains, reaching like a baby for its mother towards them, desperate to get there before the horses saw. Her hands fell on the tattered cloth they called curtains, and she was about to whip them shut when she saw them. The horses, blacker than the night, their eyes glowing a strange yellow, stood stock still. Two of them, harnessed up and pulling a cart. Ethel noticed two men, with shovels, loading the cart. When the pile was loaded, they flung the shovels on and mounted the cart themselves. As they did, one of the men, a short, stocky fella in a flat cap, darted his eyes upwards towards the window Ethel was in. She yanked the curtains closed and stood there, eyes wide open, like saucers. They had seen her. They will surely come for her now!

This is not a bedtime story told purely to get the children of Leicester off the streets and into bed before nine o'clock. It is all based on fact! Because of the terrible

trouble of the lack of a proper sewage system, people started to collect animal and human waste in piles in their garden (if they had one) or in the streets. Then, after nine o'clock, and only ever after that time due to a local law in place, farmers and farm workers would bring their horses and carts into the city to collect it. It would then be rotted down and used on the fields as fertiliser to help the crops grow. They would even pay for the more rotted-down poo, as that could be used straight away.

But why were the children scared of that, you may ask? Well, it was not unheard of for those farmers to snatch away any child wandering the streets at night. They would take them back to the farm and use them as cheap labour, having only to supply them with food, water and a bed to sleep on.

So, next time your parents tell you to go to bed or the nine o'clock horses will snatch you away, remember, it was true, not so long ago, and be grateful you are not living 150 years ago.

9

Strange Rumour and Hearsay

Many towns, cities and villages have tales of the strange and sometimes ghostly. These tales are passed on through chatter in the local pub or the family get-togethers on special occasions. Everywhere seems to have a tale or two about some spooky goings-on, and they are usually backed up by some kind of fact or half-truth. What follows is a small collection of just some of these stories that, given time, could become as well known in folklore as Black Annis herself.

South Leicestershire

In the village of Gilmorton, 10 miles south of Leicester, there are three such stories told, two of which are strikingly similar. One tells of a horse and carriage that crashed off the road between Gilmorton and Ashby Magna, on an S-bend known locally as 'Jingle-bells corner'. It is said that this carriage now haunts that road, causing many a car to swerve out of the way as the driver acts quickly to avoid the oncoming spectre. The second story recalls another carriage that crashed off the road linking the nearby village of Kimcote to the local market town of Lutterworth. This carriage, however, is said to have crashed into a small fishing pit and sank, dragging driver and passengers down with it. The wreckage was never recovered, leading locals to believe the pit was bottomless.

And finally, the third story is based very much in truth. It is the very unfortunate story of a young family who lived in a farmhouse on the Lutterworth road. The wife sadly passed away, leaving her husband to care for their daughter. He did the best he could and, still saddened greatly by the loss of his wife, managed to bring the girl up single-handedly. However, fate was not done with this family and had another cruel twist in store. One afternoon, the daughter jumped off the school bus and darted in front of it towards her father, who was waiting on the other side of the road. The bus driver failed to see the girl and, with great regret, I have to tell you that she passed away.

Not able to stand losing everyone he loved, that night the father took himself to his brick barn. He threw a coarse, thick rope over a rafter and tied a noose. That night, the poor man took his own life, and was found a few days later by a friend.

That barn is now a very expensive house, but it is still said that the father's ghost can be seen, on certain nights, walking the fields near the barn, his cries of sadness echoing all around and into the village. It is said that he looks for his wife and daughter in the afterlife but has not yet been able to find them.

Hinckley

Hinckley is a town that has a long and colourful past and, therefore, has many stories and half-truths to go with it. There are two main buildings in which strange things have been reported, though there are many others in which people have reported strange goings-on, such as the town's museum.

The first is a shop in Castle Street, the main, now pedestrianised street of the town centre. This building was built in the 1700s and became a printer's shop in the 1800s. The story goes that a young maid, who lived in the attic, fell pregnant and hid it from the family who owned the shop. Sadly, both she and the baby died during childbirth, only to be discovered the next morning. Since this tragic day, the attic has always been icy cold. Some people have reported seeing a small man wandering around. Could this be the ghost of the father? Others have reported hearing a baby cry, and some have even claimed to have seen a child running through walls. All very strange.

The second building is the Union pub. Built in the 1700s, it was said to have been used by highwaymen such as the famous Dick Turpin. This has led to sightings of a man in a black coat and a tricorn hat haunting the cellars. There is also said to be an eerie character in an old overcoat and flat cap who has been seen standing at the end of the bar. Upstairs, people have reported seeing the spirits of a man and woman. At last count, there were tales of up to five ghosts in this one public house. These are on top of the skeleton that was found during a refurbishment. Truly, many stories have been told about these spectres over the years. How many are true we will never know.

Charnwood

A truly ancient landscape is Charnwood, with rocky outcrops hiding some of the oldest fossils known to man. But these rugged lands hide more than fossils, they hide stories brought about by rumour.

One such rumour is that of the ghost of the famous nine-day queen, Lady Jane Grey. It is said that on Christmas Eve every year, she can be seen travelling in a ghostly coach from the ruins of her family home in Bradgate Park, along the road to All Saints' Church. When there, the lady disembarks, only for herself and the coach to vanish. People have also reported strange noises, voices and military drums drifting across the park.

Not far from Bradgate Park is the nineteenth-century manor house of Beaumanor Hall. There has been a hall on this site for hundreds of years, the current one being the third that we know of. So, it is not surprising to hear reports of a cavalier soldier roaming the cellar hallways with only his upper body exposed out of the ground. This would make sense as, back in the mid-1600s when the Civil War took place, the hall would have stood much lower than it does now, with the floor level being below the current cellar floor. The buildings built after this would have been built on the rubble of the previous halls.

Melton Mowbray

World-renowned for its pork pies and stilton cheese, the historic market town of Melton and its surrounding areas have many a half-truth and rumour to share. Home to many old buildings, one of the oldest is the Anne of Cleves pub on Burton Street. This building dates back to 1384, so it is bound to have a story or two about it. Among the many eerie tales of ghostly figures and ghostly dogs that brush by your leg, it is thought that the ghost of

Alfred Syetys lives there (or should I say, lived). Rumour has it that this man killed his wife in cold blood. It was said he hacked her to death with an axe. Very gruesome. Now he wanders the pub looking for his next victim!

Another pub, The Royal Oak, in the nearby village of Great Dalby, is also said to house a wicked spirit. Locals have been hit by books flying off the bookshelves, or poked by something unseen. It is generally believed to be a former landlady, Alice Johnson. Now, it is said that she was a fierce woman and stood for no nonsense. Feared by the locals, her story has been passed down and it is now thought that this ghost is hers.

Finally, on a funny note, have you ever heard the phrase 'Painting the town red'? It's a saying used for when you go out partying and having a good time. But not many people know where it comes from. Well, I can tell you that it came from Melton Mowbray. In 1837, the Marquis of Waterford, Henry de la Poer, had been hunting with the local hunt. On his return to the town, he and his friends had a few too many beers. He decided, along with his friends, that it would be terribly funny to paint many of the buildings around about bright red, so this is what they did!

You can only begin to imagine the uproar and anger from the locals the next morning, when they awoke to see their houses painted crimson red. Henry de la Poer was well known for these kinds of things – fighting, stealing, breaking windows and the like – so it is no surprise that his friends (and many others behind his back) called him 'The Mad Marquis'.

East Leicestershire

Lying on the edge of Leicester is the suburb of Scraptoft. This was once a village, before Leicester grew so big that it swallowed it up and made it part of the city. Locals still talk of the local witch, though, and her cave. If you take the footpath from Beeby Road just after the strawberry fields and walk towards the rugby club, you will see a mound in the woods on the right-hand side. If you dare to enter, you will see the roof and walls are lined with shells of all shapes and sizes. Details as to what this man-made cave is for or who built it are hard to find, so local rumour has sprung up. Now a place for local teenagers to hang out, it is also rumoured to be the home to a witch, much like Black Annis on the opposite side of town. Could it be a witch's cave? Nobody knows.

A few miles south and the countryside opens up to soft, rolling hills. The tiny hamlet of Wistow has become a well-known tourist attraction. There is now a garden centre and shops to explore, and over on the other side of the gated road is a maize maze, a seasonal maze grown out of corn every year; and every year, it is different. Carry on past these attractions and you come to a lake on one side of the road and an ancient church on the other. Legend has it that Saint Wygstan, son of King Wigmund of Mercia, is buried here. He was said to have been mercilessly murdered by an assassin, thought to be his own cousin, who whipped out a dagger from his cloak and sliced off his scalp, with his assistant driving home a sword through his gut. On the very spot where the murder happened and the scalp fell to the ground, it has been reported that, on 1 June, human hair can be found growing among the grass, even to this day. So if you visit this beautiful Norman church, remember to take your scissors, the hairy grass may need a trim.

And finally, did you know that the legendary castle fortress of Camelot can be found right here, in the rolling hills of south Leicestershire? When I was young, a man came to the door of my home in our quiet little village. He had been busy researching evidence, trying to find out where in our beautiful country the legendary King Arthur had made his home. The conclusion he had come to was that Camelot was located within Gumley. He had written a leaflet all about it, which I used my own pocket money to buy. I sat and read it through, again and again. Gumley was, and still is, my favourite part of Leicestershire, its hills dropping away towards Saddington reservoir and back towards Leicester, small spinneys and thickets dotting the landscape.

As I read the leaflet, I could see in my mind's eye the places the researcher was suggesting the mighty walls and the towering turrets of Camelot were built. I could see myself standing on that castle, looking over the ancient kingdom of Mercia with the courageous King Arthur and his beautiful queen, the fair lady Guinevere, standing by my side.

Chances are that this is not true, for Arthur probably came from Wales but, well, it's fun to think about what might have been, isn't it?

10

Lady Jane Grey

Can you imagine being king? Can you even begin to think about what it would be like to rule a whole country, with every important decision having to be made by you? Surely, this is a tough job for even the most well-educated and experienced adult. Now, imagine you were king and you were only 9 years old. I am guessing that some of you reading this are 9 years old or around that age (and if you're not, you can remember being that old). At the age of 9, most children are playing with their friends, going to school to learn new things and just being a child. Not Edward VI.

Edward VI was the son of the famous Henry VIII. His mother was Jane Seymour, Henry's third wife, who, if you remember the rhyme, died just after giving birth to her son. In 1547, when Edward was only 9 years old, he found himself without a mother or father and with a crown on his head, now King of England. He was in charge. He called the shots. It was all up to him now.

This was hard for Edward. He had a team of advisors to help him, whispering advice into his ears at every opportunity. As he was not old enough to actually rule, these advisors, his council, were the real power. Edward was just the face of the crown. He tried his best until 1553, when he became ill. Doctors and healers from across the land were brought to see him but they all stood there, stroking their long beards, shaking their heads. The boy king was going to die, and nobody could stop it.

Edward, and more so the high council, began to worry as to who would become king or queen next. Edward was too young to have children of his own, so who was it going to be? He had a special order written up called a 'Devise for the succession'. This named someone quite surprising as the next ruler of England.

Meanwhile, in a large walled garden, wrapped up by rolling hills and craggy outcrops, stood a rather magnificent house. Here, in the centre of the deer park we know today as Bradgate Park, lived the young girl Lady Jane Grey. She was born at the beginning of 1537 and grew up surrounded by the beautiful countryside of north-west Leicestershire. She was taught well by many tutors, and much preferred to stay inside reading than going riding or hunting. Her education was considered the best there was in the land. In fact, Jane even said that she could not do anything, not even eating or drinking, for fear of being told off by her parents. She had to be perfect at all times. Can you imagine that, having to be perfect at everything you do, all the time?

Lady Jane longed to be free of this but did not want to move away from her home, for it was in her heart and soul. She belonged to Bradgate and it to her. However, when she was 9 years old, she was sent away to live with the uncle of King Edward VI, a man called Thomas Seymour. She was only there for a year and a half when Thomas's wife died giving birth. This saw Jane sent back to her beloved home of Bradgate.

Not long after, though, Jane found herself back at Thomas's house for a few months, where she learnt of plans for her to marry King Edward. Jane's head began to spin. The king was her second cousin, but that was alright, she thought. She would become queen! She would sit next to the king and rule England! This was exciting at first, and Jane had visions of ruling, but then she began to imagine all the bad things, the weight of ruling, the threat of being assassinated by someone who wanted the throne themselves or of all-out war. The more

Jane thought of it, the more she realised that being queen was not for her, so it came as a relief when this did not happen. She, instead, became engaged to Lord Guildford Dudley, in 1553. His father was not a king but head of the council that ruled for the king. Jane's soon-to-be father-in-law was the most powerful man in the country, even more powerful than the king.

Jane found herself to be very lonely in these times. She was now in her teens and longed for friends. She wanted to be with girls her own age, to talk about life, boys and to laugh and giggle, but she was not allowed. Her life was too important to others. Not long after she got engaged, on 10 July, Lady Jane Grey, the second cousin of Edward VI, was officially proclaimed queen.

Her second cousin, King Edward VI, had passed away on 6 July and with his passing, the 'Devise for the succession' made sure Lady Jane Grey became queen. News of this reached Jane on 9 July and it was made official the day after. She was queen. Edward was 15 when he died, Jane was but a year older. She did not want this. She did not want to be queen, yet it was thrust upon her. There were others that could or should have been queen. Her cousins, Edward's half-sisters, Mary and Elizabeth, were not named queen as they were Catholics and Edward was a Protestant, two different forms of Christianity. This may seem silly to you now, but half a century ago, what you believed in was a matter of life and death.

And so it was for Jane. She and her new husband, who she refused to name king, moved to the Tower of London, where they were to stay until the coronation which would make her title official. However, after only nine days as queen, poor Jane, so young and so clever, found herself overthrown by those that plotted against her and they named Mary as the real Queen of England. Mary had not been captured and was able to gather her supporters. Even Jane's father-in-law, realising he could not win the battle against Mary and her supporters, switched sides.

On 19 July, Jane found herself being led, in chains, to the tower of her new home, the Tower of London. There she stayed, crying herself to sleep, night after night, unsure of her fate. What would become of her? She never wanted this. She never wanted to be queen. She dreamt of those days of her childhood spent in Bradgate. She remembered watching the herds of deer moving like clouds over the hillside. She longed to be back to see the forests tumbling over the hills, the rocky outcrops like the bony fists of a giant, bursting out of the sea of green. All that was now a distant memory, replaced by the stinking streets of London, the stench of the foul water of the River Thames and the echoing sounds of 'Gardyloo' as people threw their toilet waste out of their windows onto the streets below.

A trial was held later in the year of 1553, and Jane was found guilty of high treason. The

penalty: death by execution. Jane broke down when the verdict was found. She had never wanted any of this! It was she who said she should not be queen. It was not her doing. This was not fair, she thought. However, the execution was not carried out until her father and brother took part in an uprising, trying to stop the new Queen Mary from marrying Prince Philip of Spain.

With her father and brother proving to be a threat to Queen Mary, it was thought it was too dangerous for Jane to be alive. On 12 February 1554, being only around 17 years old, Jane found herself kneeling at the executioner's block. She asked the executioner if he could do it before she had to rest her head on the block, but he refused. Jane blindfolded herself and leant forward. She was shaking with fear and, in her blindfolded state, could not find the block to rest her head. She cried out in fear for help. When she had been helped onto the block she said a brief prayer before the axe fell and

was followed by the eternal sleep. In her last moment, she thought once more of her home and all its beauty.

Many, many years later, the park and the ruins of Lady Jane Grey's house were left in trust to the people of Leicestershire. Following this, landowners from neighbouring areas added more land to create the park we know today. So, next time you are in the park, scrabbling over those ancient rocks, hiding in the timeworn oak trees, paddling in the river or walking past the ruins in Bradgate Park, spare a thought for that scared little girl, not even an adult, who became queen by chance, and lost her life because of it. She called that place home and deserves to be remembered.

11

The Bleeding Gravestone

The 1700s were a complicated time for our royalty. At the start of the century, two Acts (laws) were made to stop any Catholics from sitting on the throne. This meant that only those who were Protestants could rule Great Britain. All this meant was that the parliament at the time, the people we have who run the country, not the king or queen, wanted a Protestant monarch (see, I told you it was confusing, keep up). Back then it was not as simple as the prince becoming king. With this, it meant that twenty potential kings and queens missed out on sitting on the throne! The crown eventually fell to a German called George. When he died, the crown passed to his son, who became George II. There were some arguments during his reign as to who should really be king and, after the last battle in which an English king led his troops, George II's main contender to the throne, his son, died nine years before his father. This meant that George II's grandson, another George, became king, making him George III. Are you confused? I think I am …

Anyway, now you know a little bit about the confusing times this story is set in, I can get on with telling you the tale.

It was April 1727. George I was still clinging on to the throne and to his life. He was 67 and struggling. The army had been sent out across the land to recruit good, strong young men, as there were still arguments over who should be king, and many believed it should not be a

German like George. On this fateful day, the army marched into Hinckley.

The sergeant of the troops stood atop a box in the middle of the market. He began preaching to the crowds about how great the army was, how they could earn a decent wage and do right for their country and king. People began to gather. Very few believed the words coming out of the sergeant's mouth, but they listened all the same. He proceeded to order the troops to give the crowd demonstrations of how they could use their weapons in battle, and the crowd 'oohh'd' and 'ahhh'd' as metal clanked against metal and swords and spears swung through the air.

When the demonstrations were over, the sergeant, now standing holding a long halberd (a mix between a spear and a battleaxe), began to preach on how all Catholics were bad and what they believed in was wrong. The only way they could make amends for their faith was to join the army and fight for King George, or so

he said. This angered some of the crowd and they began shouting back at the sergeant.

A handsome young man, Richard Smith, was leaning with his back on a tree when he shouted that, 'Not all Catholics are bad!'

The sergeant's head swivelled to look at this young man. 'You should do less with your mouth and more with your hands,' he sneered, 'why don't you pick up a weapon, join us and defend your king. After all, you drink in the pub that carries his name, celebrating his true greatness.' The sergeant motioned towards the inn.

Richard sniggered, his shoulders shook and then he began to laugh, managing to say, 'It is named the George after the mighty Saint George who slew the dragon, not after a fat German who pretends to be king!'

This angered the sergeant so much that he cried, 'Well now then everyone, you shall see one more demonstration, how a halberd works!'

He took the halberd and rammed it straight through the stomach of Richard, and into the tree behind, so hard that the sergeant had to raise his foot and brace it against the tree in order to free the halberd. When it was pulled out, it tore a hole in Richard's stomach and the crowd watched on in horror as they saw his insides become outsides.

The sergeant and his men, knowing they had outstayed their welcome, packed up and left, leaving Richard as a warning to all those who saw.

Richard was buried in St Mary's churchyard, and on his gravestone they engraved:

A fatal Halbert his mortal Body slew,
The murdering Hand God's vengeance
    will pursue.
From shades Terrestrial, though Justice
    took her flight,
Shall not the judge of all the Earth do
    right.
Each Age and Sex his Innocence bemoans
And with sad sighs laments his dying
    Groans.

This tells of Richard's last act and how God will seek justice for his death. And now, it is said

that on the day of his death, 12 April, every year, his gravestone bleeds. Beads of red liquid run down the gravestone as it weeps tears of blood in memory of Richard Smith.

So, next time you're in Hinckley, take a walk among the ancient trees, through the

gravestones, avoiding the many squirrels and pigeons, towards the play park – but keep an eye out for Richard's grave, as it might be 12 April and you might see his tears of blood.

12

Shag-Dog

The River Soar snakes through Leicester and on through the Soar Valley, through little villages, skirting Loughborough, becoming the boundary line between Leicestershire and Nottinghamshire before joining the River Trent at the spot where three counties – Leicestershire, Derbyshire and Nottinghamshire – meet. This river has been the lifeblood of Leicester and was made into a river canal in the late 1700s. This brought canal barges to Leicester and the north of the county. With it came lots of trade – wool, fabrics, coal and many, many more types of cargo. Alongside this, it also brought the men that worked on these barges. These, the people called Bargees. They were rough men who worked hard but were often in trouble with the locals or the law. This scared the people of the villages that sat on the once-peaceful riverbanks.

In Birstall, there was a place called Shag-Dog Pit. This was said to be home to a giant, black hound and people would stay well clear of it. Nobody was sure as to whether this beast was friend or foe. However, one dark night they found out.

It was the early 1800s and a young girl was sitting by her best friend's bedside. Her friend was sick. The fever had lasted many days and she had started to become worried. No amount of care and love would help her friend now. A doctor was needed.

It was getting late, so the young girl set off on the walk to the nearest doctor's house. He lived just over a mile away in the nearby village of Belgrave. The quickest, easiest route for the young girl was along the canal path. The sun was still up and so she felt safe on the journey there. When she arrived, she spoke with the doctor, who gave her some advice and a draught for her friend to take, and he said he would be there first thing in the morning.

By the time the girl left the doctor's house, the sun had set. Dusk had begun to fall. She set off along the canal path, heading back towards her friend's house. She was on a familiar stretch of towpath and she knew home was nearby. Night had fallen, the blanket of darkness had draped over the land. It was a dark night for the girl to be walking with only the light of the stars and her knowledge of the way home to guide her.

Mist had rolled out along the river now, muffling the sounds of her footsteps. As she strained her ears for any sounds to help her find her way, she heard footsteps that were not her own. She paused and turned her head. There was a light behind her in the gloom. Cutting through the mist, she could see a shadow of a man. He wore a cap and baggy clothes and was stumbling towards her. She knew he was a Bargee, and that he meant no good. A young girl on her own at night was a prime target to be robbed, and no mistake, she knew this. Her head spun back around and she quickened her pace.

She glanced around again to see the man getting ever closer. It was at this point that she felt something large by her side. She continued walking for fear of the pursuer. As she walked she could feel the heat of a warm body and breath on her legs. Instantly, she knew what this was. She had heard tales of this creature, but she still had to look down to be sure.

She was right. There, by her side, padding silently through the mist with her, was a dog. This was not any dog, though. It was huge. This dog's shoulders came up to the girl's hips. Its fur was as black as shadows. Even in the darkness, she could still see its muscles rippling beneath its skin. It glanced at her and that's when she saw its eyes glowed red. No pupils, just a faint red glow. This would normally scare the young girl half to death, but not this night. She felt no fear. All she felt was calm and safety. The huge dog padded alongside her until she turned off the towpath and down the lane to her friend's house. She was safe. She had never thought to look back at her pursuer.

The next morning, true to his word, the doctor arrived and administered some more medicine to the girl's friend, and the girl retold the story of her journey to him.

'Interesting,' replied the doctor. 'You see, on my way here I passed an empty barge. Then another, but with people talking inside. I only heard snippets of the conversation, but it seemed the Bargee who owned the now abandoned barge had not been seen all night or morning.'

The story and the news of the missing Bargee spread. People began to put two and two together and started making their own minds up. However, from that day, the people of Birstall had no trouble from the Bargee folk, in fact, they sailed right on by, choosing to moor up elsewhere for the night in fear of the Shag-Dog from the Shag-Dog Pit.

13

Dick Turpin

Have you heard of highwaymen? These men were kind of like land pirates. They became famous in the seventeenth and eighteenth centuries. Up and down the highways and byways of the land they would ride, wearing tricorn hats and long trench coats, just like pirates, but on horses not ships. They would hold up and rob carriages before riding off into the night with their loot. Just as with pirates, it was seen to be a fun thing to be, a dandy highwayman, robbing the rich and living a life of danger and excitement.

The most infamous of all these highwaymen was Dick Turpin. Many stories, songs and poems have been written about this man. It was said that he was handsome, noble and brave, robbing the rich and sharing his treasure with the poor, much like the beloved Robin Hood of Nottingham. In truth, though, Dick Turpin was nothing like this. His is a violent story and one that passes through Leicestershire thanks to an ancient road on the south-west side of the county.

Richard Turpin was born in Essex in 1705, and became a butcher when he grew up, just like his dear old dad. He worked hard, fell in love, got married and finally got his own butcher's shop. Life was good. However – and you knew this was coming – things changed. He fell in with the wrong crowd. He became friends with a bunch of criminals calling themselves Gregory's Gang. Dick, as he was now known, began robbing and thieving deer from the forests. This, back in the early 1700s, was a serious crime. He soon realised that thieving made him more money than being a butcher, so he did it more and more. He was good at it, really good! But the rest of the gang, not so good. They all ended up getting caught and Dick ran away.

For the next few years he disappeared, with reports of him now being a highwayman spreading across the land. He was said to have

been ruthless, not afraid to shoot and kill anyone who didn't hand over their money or precious items. It was during this time that he ended up in Leicestershire.

The stories tell of Dick Turpin moving in with his parents, who had relocated to a small village in Fenny Drayton, about 7 miles north of Hinckley. From there he would ride out to Watling Street, an old Roman road stretching from London to North Wales, now known as the A5. He would ride up and down the road, tricorn hat on head, face covered by a black scarf and his trench coat flapping in the wind behind him, his trusty horse, Black Bess, carrying him swiftly along. There were reports of the rogue all the way up to Lichfield and beyond. The locals all knew who he was and the terrible things he had done and was still doing. So why did they not tell the local authorities and have him arrested?

That was simple. Dick Turpin would buy their silence with beer. He would drink at a local tavern called The Cock Inn at Sibson, which is still there to this day and is now the second oldest pub in the country, built in 1250. Whilst drinking there, Dick would use the money he had robbed to buy the locals beer. The more he bought them, the less likely they were to tell anyone that the infamous Dick Turpin had been there. In fact, he felt so safe there that when the authorities came looking for him he would ride to that pub, put Black Bess in the cellar with the beer, and he would hide in the chimney and nobody would say a word.

Legend has it that Dick Turpin was a handsome rogue, looking out for the poor and for his friends. In truth, he'd had a terrible, but very common, disease when he was younger, called smallpox. This had left his face covered in scars. He was once described by a newspaper as 'about 5ft 9ins high, brown complexion, very much marked with the smallpox, his cheek bones broad, his face thinner towards the bottom, his visage short, pretty upright and pretty broad about the shoulders'. He was, as I have said, not very nice. He even ended up shooting and killing one of his best friends! This was by accident, or so he claimed, but still, that wasn't very nice at all.

Not long after he shot his friend, in 1737, Dick shot a man called Thomas Morris, who was trying to capture him. Thomas was quite an important man and Dick knew this. He panicked and rode north to hide out in Yorkshire. Once there, he changed his name to John Palmer and tried to stay out of sight of those trying to hunt him down. This didn't work.

There was now a nationwide search for the famous highwayman, and Dick (or John, as he was now) was scared. He knew this would happen one day but had chosen not to think about it. Now he was hiding in fear of his life. There was a big problem, though: Dick … I mean John, didn't

know how to hide. He liked being bold and brash and the centre of attention. The final mistake he made was shooting his landlord's chicken and threatening to shoot him too. The local constable in Bough, near Hull, where all this happened, arrested John Palmer and he was sent to Beverley House of Correction, a kind of jail. He wasn't there long before he was found out to be a horse thief, having stolen some horses whilst he was trying to hide out as John Palmer (I told you he wasn't very good at hiding). This crime was more serious than shooting a chicken, so he was moved to a bigger, scarier prison: York Castle.

Now, this is where the story gets really interesting. You see, John … erm, Dick … or is it still John at this point, I forget … anyway, he had a bit of real bad luck. John/Dick, whoever he was, made a massive mistake. He wrote a letter to his brother-in-law, his sister's husband, back in Essex. When it got there, it was returned to the local post house as he hadn't paid for it to be delivered. His brother-in-law refused to pay the sixpence to receive it, so it was returned. Nothing bad yet, I hear you say, but wait. Would you believe it, working at the post house was a man who used to be a schoolmaster, teaching the local children how to write, a man by the name of James Smith. When James Smith, the postmaster, saw the letter he instantly recognised the handwriting. He had taught Dick Turpin to write and was certain that this letter was from the infamous highwayman himself!

James Smith turned the letter over to the authorities, who managed to put two and two together and realised that John Palmer, the horse thief, was in fact Dick Turpin, highwayman extraordinaire!

Dick was then sentenced and found guilty of his crimes. The punishment was for him to be hung by the neck until dead.

On the morning of 7 April 1739, the dandy highwayman, Dick Turpin, strode towards his fate. He had bought a new coat and shoes for the occasion. Well, you only get to die once, so you may as well look good doing it, he thought. Over 500 people turned out to catch sight of this famous outlaw. Through the streets of York he rode, in an open cart, people booing him all around. Dick walked steadily up to the rope. He showed no signs of fear, although his right leg started to shake as he climbed the ladder. The noose was placed around his neck and tightened. Dick turned to the topsman, the man who would do the deed, and spoke a few words into his ear before jumping off the barrel himself. He was a showman until his last breath, which took five minutes to come, his body hanging there in front of the crowd.

Dick Turpin's story crosses the country, from south to north, but he will always be remembered in Leicestershire and up and down Watling Street. In fact, there have been reports, even to this day, of drivers seeing a ghostly figure wearing a tricorn hat and trench coat, face covered, riding a black horse, charging up and down the A5 where the Harrow Brook crosses under the road. There was once a pub there, but it is now a roundabout and an industrial estate. Maybe Dick Turpin is searching for some treasure from a robbery that he buried near the stream, who knows, but one thing is for sure: he made certain his legend lives on for many, many years.

14

King Richard III: the Myth, the Legend, the Truth

When I was a schoolboy (which wasn't that long ago, honest), I remember going on a school trip into Leicester. We got off the coach outside a large, white building and I read the big, black words on the wall. We were at Newarke Houses Museum. I loved museums, places full of things to explore and stories to discover, so I remember I skipped in full of excitement.

My classmates and I spent the morning exploring. There was loads to see. We looked at all the old toys that our parents and grandparents would have played with when they were our age, we explored the recreated Victorian street with shops and a pub, and even dared to brave the First World War trench, with its explosions and flashing lights. However, the exhibit that stuck in my mind the most that morning was the one about Daniel Lambert, the fattest man alive at the turn of the nineteenth century. They had his chair and his trousers, which were massive!

At lunch, I remember having tomato ketchup sandwiches (try them, they're delicious!), before we headed out of the museum for a walk. I had only ever been to the shopping area in Leicester, so I had no idea there was anywhere else to explore. I never liked going into Leicester. We only ever went once a year, at Christmas, to do the Christmas shopping. It was always wet and cold, with thousands of people hustling and bustling all around, buildings towering high over me, blocking out any light that tried to burst through the thick rain clouds, and neon lights glaring out of shop windows accompanied by cheesy Christmas songs. I grew up in a quiet little village with fields, trees, grass and peace. I didn't like Leicester at all. Little did I know that this walk was about to open my eyes and change my mind for good.

We headed down to the banks of the River Soar, the very same river that had been turned into a canal many years ago and, a few miles north, had the Shag-Dog prowling its shores, protecting those in need. When we got onto the towpath next to the river, I noticed the quiet. I stood for a minute and listened and heard, at last, the sounds I was used to. I heard the wind in the trees, the birds singing and the coo-ing of the coots and the moorhens on the water. The spring sunshine fell through the leaves and danced on the softly rippling surface of the water, disturbed only by the occasional rowing boat, drifting by, from the local university. I breathed in deeply and smiled.

We walked along the towpath for a short while until we came to a bridge. The teacher then told us all about it. It was called Bow Bridge and dated back hundreds of years. We were told the story of King Richard III. We were told how he was an evil king, locking his nephews, the rightful heirs to the throne, in the Tower of London and then having them murdered so that he, Richard, could be king. We stood listening in awe to tales of the battles he fought against Henry Tudor in the Wars of the Roses, battles fought around the Midlands, near us, all to decide who should be king. Then the teacher told us of his final battle and the importance of the Bow Bridge.

It was said that King Richard III stayed in the Blue Boar Inn the night before his final battle. In the morning, he saddled his horse, donned his armour, and led his army out of Leicester, heading west to meet Henry Tudor once more, hoping this time the argument would be settled once and for all. As he rode over the Bow Bridge, the spur on his heel struck a stone on the bridge, about a metre from the

ground. At that point, an old hag, cloaked in black, with a strange blue glow from under her hood (does she sound familiar?) stepped out in front of him. She spoke to all that would listen and foretold that on his return into the city, Richard's head would hit that very same stone. Well, this was silly! Why would Richard's head be that low? Everyone laughed this off and pushed the hag aside, who then disappeared into the crowd.

On his march to battle, Richard could not help but think about what the hag had said. He took it as a good omen. He would be returning to the city and surely that would mean victory or, at the very least, he would still be alive.

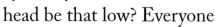

Somewhere near the village of Stoke Golding, King Richard III and his forces came face to face with the rival to the throne, Henry Tudor, and his followers. Richard's army was bigger but there was one piece of the puzzle yet to fall into place. The Stanleys had a large force of men but were undecided as to who to fight for. They held back and watched what happened.

Richard's forces charged at Henry's and, for a time, seemed to have the upper hand, but then things started to go wrong. Richard's commanders missed some vital commands and didn't charge. Some of his men panicked and fled, and Richard made a desperate move. Seeing Henry was exposed, his forces stretched, Richard led his royal guards on a charge to kill Henry once and for all.

The Stanleys, watching from afar, saw this and saw Richard was now vulnerable. The traitors, who had once bowed in support of the king, now surrounded him and his guards and helped cut them down, killing Richard and ending the Plantagenet line of kings.

The battle was over, the war was won, Henry was crowned king under an oak tree in Stoke Golding. 'But what of Richard's body?' I remember someone calling out. 'And what about him banging his head when he came back?' someone else asked. The teacher then told us how Richard was stripped naked and flung over a horse. He was brought back into Leicester, so the people could see he was dead and, as he crossed the Bow Bridge, his head hung so low that, as told by the lady in black, it hit the very same stone as his spur had.

A plaque was on the bridge and the teacher read it. It explained how the evil King Richard's body was buried, only to have his bones dug up years later and tossed into the river where he lay, even to that day.

What a story! I never knew Leicester was so interesting! I never knew this was the place of battles, dead kings and stories to make your head spin!

I grew up thinking I knew the story of the evil King Richard III and his death, and how he now sleeps with the fishes in the river but, one day, as I was driving, listening to BBC Radio Leicester, my ears pricked up. They were reporting on a local dig in the city. The archaeologists (people who dig up the ground to find things from long ago) had begun digging in a car park and had found a body, underneath where there was painted an 'R' from the word 'Parking'. Everybody started saying how amazing it would be if this was King Richard III, but his bones were in the river, we all knew that. And anyway, there are thousands of bodies in the ground from long, long ago, it would be like finding a needle in a haystack, but the whole world started to pay attention to our city.

As the days ticked by, they slowly uncovered the body. The spine was bent, just like Richard's

had been. The bones were of the right age. Could it be? No, surely not.

A distant living ancestor of King Richard was found, an American carpenter, from whom scientists took some DNA (the thing that makes you you, passed down from your parents) to see if this could prove that this was the skeleton of Richard.

The news finally broke that yes, the bones found under the letter 'R', in a car park, were those of the long-lost king, Richard III, the last King of England to die in battle. Leicester became world-famous. The news spread to all corners of the world. More and more people began to investigate his story and more and more people started to question if he was evil or just misunderstood.

On 26 March 2015, King Richard III, the last Plantagenet king, was laid to rest in a coffin made by one of his descendants, in Leicester Cathedral. He lies there still, waiting for you to come and see him and tell him your stories. And whilst you're here in this wonderful county, full of stories of giants, witches, demon dogs and much, much more, take the time to look around you, find these stories and maybe more. Everywhere has a story to tell. I have only told you a few, now it's your turn to find the rest.

Happy story hunting, my friends.

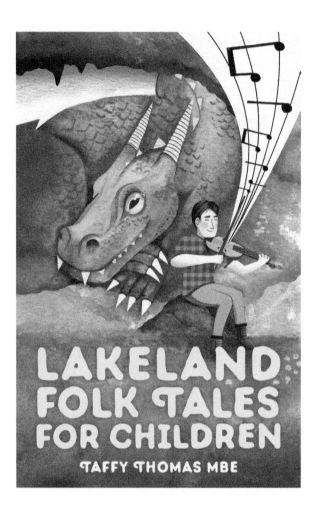

LAKELAND FOLK TALES FOR CHILDREN

TAFFY THOMAS MBE

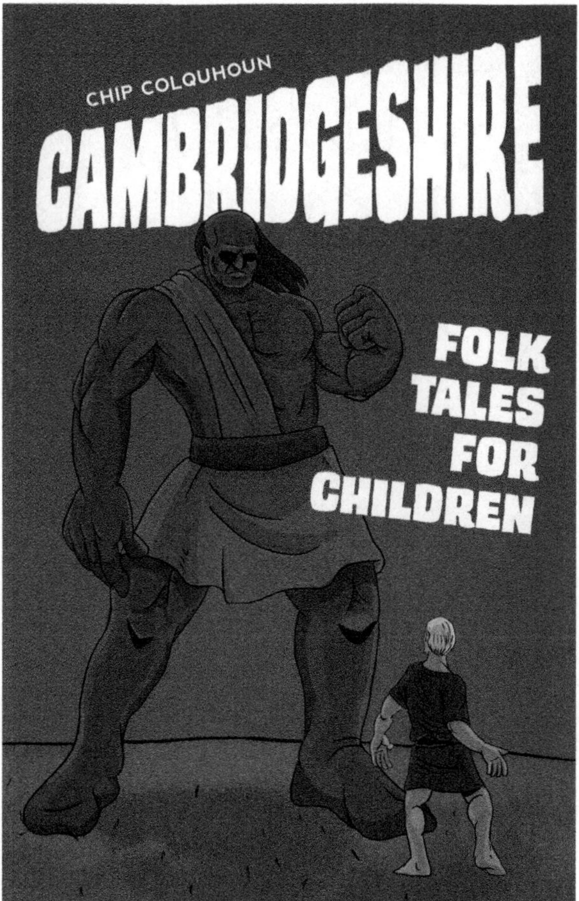
CHIP COLQUHOUN
CAMBRIDGESHIRE
FOLK TALES FOR CHILDREN

DERBYSHIRE
FOLK
TALES

P E T E   C A S T L E

Society *for*
Storytelling

Since 1993, The Society for Storytelling has championed the ancient art of oral storytelling and its long and honourable history – not just as entertainment, but also in education, health, and inspiring and changing lives. Storytellers, enthusiasts and academics support and are supported by this registered charity to ensure the art is nurtured and developed throughout the UK.

Many activities of the Society are available to all, such as locating storytellers on the Society website, taking part in our annual National Storytelling Week at the start of every February, purchasing our quarterly magazine Storylines, or attending our Annual Gathering – a chance to revel in engaging performances, inspiring workshops, and the company of like-minded people.

You can also become a member of the Society to support the work we do. In return, you receive free access to Storylines, discounted tickets to the Annual Gathering and other storytelling events, the opportunity to join our mentorship scheme for new storytellers, and more. Among our great deals for members is a 30% discount off titles from The History Press.

For more information, including how to join, please visit

www.sfs.org.uk